All children have a great ambition to read to themselves... and a sense of achievement when they can do so.

*The **read it yourself** series has been devised to satisfy their ambition. Even before children begin to learn to read formally, perhaps using a reading scheme, it is important that they have books and stories which will actively encourage the development of essential pre-reading skills. Books at Level 1 in this series have been devised with this in mind and will supplement pre-reading books available in any reading scheme.*

Based on well-known nursery rhymes and games which children will have heard, these simple pre-readers introduce key words and phrases which children will meet in later reading. Many young children will remember the words rather than read them but this is a normal part of pre-reading.

In this book, accompanying the rhyme, there is a text for the children to read and an adult text, which asks questions encouraging children to think about the rhyme and look more closely at the pictures. It is recommended that the parent or teacher should read the book aloud to the child first and then go through the story, with the child reading the text and answering the questions.

British Library Cataloguing in Publication Data
Murdock, Hy
    There was an old woman who swallowed a fly.
    1. Nursery rhymes in English
    I. Title   II. Burton, Terry   III. Series
    398'8
    ISBN 0-7214-1266-1

First edition

Published by Ladybird Books Ltd Loughborough Leicestershire UK
Ladybird Books Inc Auburn Maine 04210 USA

There was an old woman who swallowed a fly

by Hy Murdock
illustrated by Terry Burton

Ladybird Books

This old woman is in her garden.

How many animals can you see in the picture?

*There was an old woman
   who swallowed a fly.
I don't know why
   she swallowed a fly.
Perhaps she'll die.*

Here is a fly.

How many wings does the fly have?

*There was an old woman
who swallowed a spider
That wriggled and jiggled
and tickled inside her.*

This is a spider.

Count the spider's legs.

She swallowed the spider
to catch the fly.
I don't know why
she swallowed a fly.
Perhaps she'll die.

The old
woman is
laughing.

*Are you
ticklish?*

*There was an old woman
    who swallowed a bird.
How absurd,
    to swallow a bird!*

There are some birds in this tree.

Which bird is singing?

Here is a cat with her kittens.

Do you like milk?

The old woman
swallowed the fly.
The spider chased
the fly.
The bird chased
the spider.
The cat chased
the bird.

Here are some dogs.
They are playing.

Which is the brown and white dog?

There are five cows in the field.

How many cows are lying down?

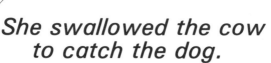

*She swallowed the cow
to catch the dog.
She swallowed the dog
to catch the cat.
She swallowed the cat
to catch the bird.
She swallowed the bird
to catch the spider.
She swallowed the spider
to catch the fly.*

Look at the animals.

Which animals did the old woman swallow?

*There was an old woman
who swallowed a horse.*

This is a horse.

She's dead of course!

The rhyme

There was an old woman who swallowed a fly.
I don't know why she swallowed a fly.
Perhaps she'll die.

There was an old woman who swallowed a spider
That wriggled and jiggled and tickled inside her.
She swallowed the spider to catch the fly.
I don't know why she swallowed a fly.
Perhaps she'll die.

There was an old woman who swallowed a bird.
How absurd, to swallow a bird!
She swallowed the bird to catch the spider... etc.

There was an old woman who swallowed a cat.
Well, fancy that, she swallowed a cat!
She swallowed the cat to catch the bird... etc.

There was an old woman who swallowed a dog.
What a hog, to swallow a dog!
She swallowed the dog to catch the cat... etc.

There was an old woman who swallowed a cow.
I don't know how she swallowed a cow!
She swallowed the cow to catch the dog.
She swallowed the dog to catch the cat.
She swallowed the cat to catch the bird.
She swallowed the bird to catch the spider
That wriggled and jiggled and tickled inside her.
She swallowed the spider to catch the fly.
I don't know why she swallowed a fly.
Perhaps she'll die.

There was an old woman who swallowed a horse.
She's dead of course!

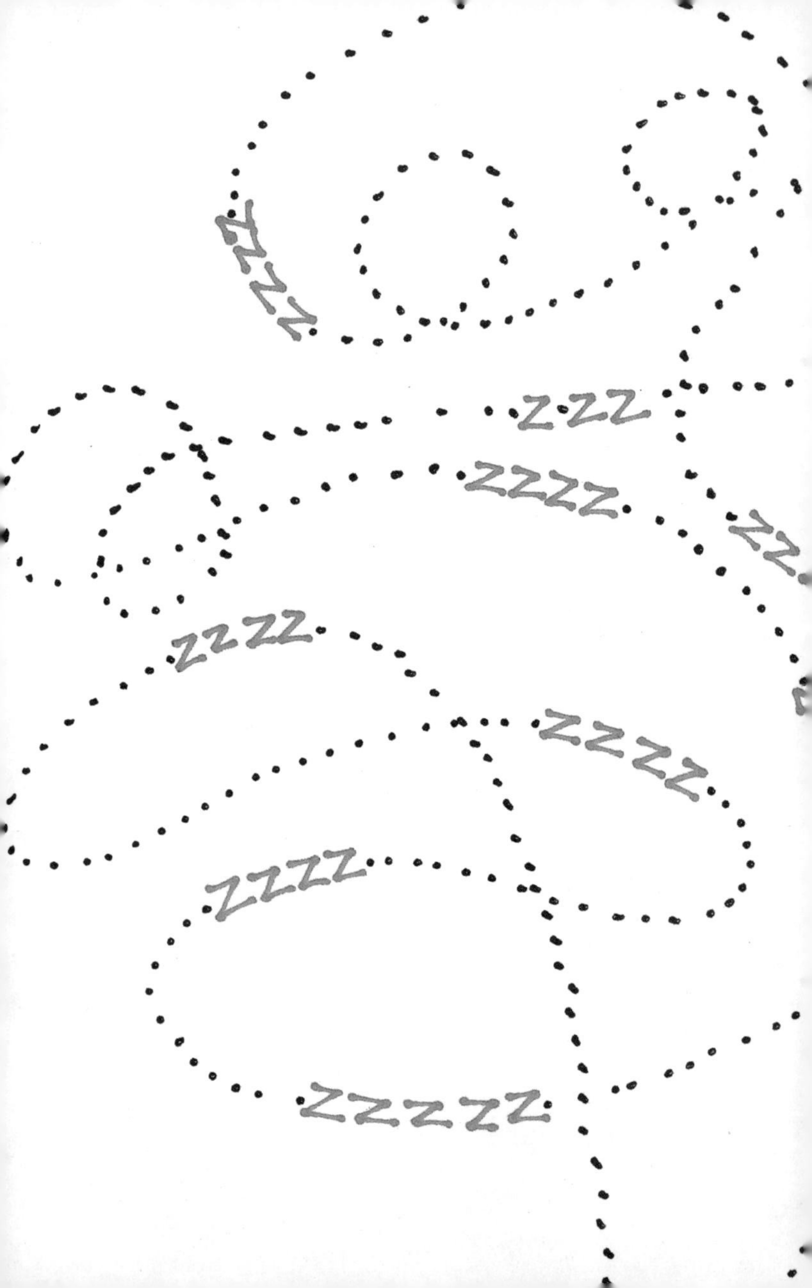
ZZZZ
ZZZ
ZZZZ
ZZ
ZZZZ
ZZZZ
ZZZZ
ZZZZZ